WELCOME TO
PASSPORT TO READING
A beginning reader's ticket to a brand-new world!

Every book in this program is designed to build read-along and read-alone skills, level by level, through engaging and enriching stories. As the reader turns each page, he or she will become more confident with new vocabulary, sight words, and comprehension.

These PASSPORT TO READING levels will help you choose the perfect book for every reader.

READING TOGETHER
Read short words in simple sentence structures together to begin a reader's journey.

READING OUT LOUD
Encourage developing readers to sound out words in more complex stories with simple vocabulary.

READING INDEPENDENTLY
Newly independent readers gain confidence reading more complex sentences with higher word counts.

READY TO READ MORE
Readers prepare for chapter books with fewer illustrations and longer paragraphs.

This book features sight words from the educator-supported Dolch Sight Words List. This encourages the reader to recognize commonly used vocabulary words, increasing reading speed and fluency.

For more information, please visit www.passporttoreadingbooks.com, where each reader can add stamps to a personalized passport while traveling through story after story!

Enjoy the journey!

Little, Brown and Company

Hachette Book Group
237 Park Avenue, New York, NY 10017
Visit our website at www.lb-kids.com

Little, Brown and Company is a division of Hachette Book Group, Inc.
The Little, Brown name and logo are trademarks of Hachette Book Group, Inc.

The publisher is not responsible for websites (or their content) that are not owned by the publisher.

First Edition: October 2011

ISBN 978-0-316-18297-3

10 9 8 7 6 5 4 3 2 1

CW

Printed in the United States of America

I Am Kermit the Frog

Adapted by Ray Santos
Based on the screenplay
by Jason Segel & Nick Stoller
illustrated by Stephan Britt
and Steve James

L B

LITTLE, BROWN AND COMPANY
Boston   New York

Hi, ho, Muppet fans!

Can you find these things in this book?

BANJO

GOWN

MANSION

A young green frog named Kermit

sat on a lily pad in a swamp,

listening to the birds singing pretty songs.

He wanted to make music like that, too.

So Kermit picked up a banjo

and made music all day long.

He also taught himself how to dance.

The other animals in the swamp

loved Kermit's music.

Even the snakes smiled.

Kermit decided to spend his life

making others happy with songs and dance.

Kermit heard of a place called Hollywood.

People there performed and made movies.

Movies made lots of people happy.

Kermit decided to leave the swamp

and follow his dream.

He packed some flies for the trip.

Kermit stopped in a small town.
There was an open talent show,
and up onstage was Fozzie Bear.
"Why are fish so smart?" Fozzie asked.
"Because they swim in schools! Wocka! Wocka!"
No one laughed at the joke.

Kermit felt bad for the bear,
but he also admired his courage.
"Do you want to come to Hollywood?"
Kermit asked him.
"Wow! Yes," answered Fozzie.
"But I have one question:
What is a Hollywood?"

Traveling across the country,
Kermit and Fozzie met more friends,
who all loved to perform.
They all shared Kermit's dream
to make people happy.
As they got closer and closer to Hollywood,
the group got bigger and bigger.

They stopped for gas
just before they reached Hollywood.
Kermit heard someone singing
and followed the voice until he found a pig.
Miss Piggy could sing well,
and she was also very good
at wearing sparkling gowns and heels.

Kermit had never seen a pig like her before,
and it was love at first sight for Piggy!
Miss Piggy joined their merry band.
She always wanted to be a star—a big star!
She thought Kermit could make that happen.

Finally, the gang arrived!

They called themselves the Muppets.

They sang, danced, and made people happy.

And then it happened!

The Muppets became rich and famous!

Their showbiz dreams came true!

"Kermie, we are stars," Piggy said.

"Stars go in the sky," said Kermit.

"We are just lucky."

Nearby, Gonzo shot himself out of a cannon
and soared into the air over their heads.

"Well, okay, maybe Gonzo is a star,"
joked Kermit.

For years the Muppets performed together
at their own Muppet Studios!
Kermit directed them in movies,
a television show,
and even a Broadway musical!
"Yaaaaay!" cheered Kermit.
He was his friends' biggest fan.

The Muppets knew he would not let them down!

Kermit made sure everything went well.

Funny jokes! Amazing stunts! Wonderful songs!

Kermit was one very busy frog.

Miss Piggy loved Kermit a lot.

He cared for her, too.

But Kermit was so busy putting on shows,

he had no time to spend with her.

Finally, Miss Piggy grew angry.

They had a fight and she decided to leave.

"Bye, Kermie," she said.

She left the Muppets.

Without her, it just was not the same.

The other Muppets decided to go, too.

There was nothing Kermit could do.

Years passed, but the Muppets still had fans.
Two of them, Walter and Gary,
made their own special trip to Hollywood.
They wanted to see the Muppet Studios,
the home of their heroes!

When they got to Hollywood,
Walter and Gary found out
that the Muppets' theater
was going to be torn down.
They had to find some way to save it!
Walter and Gary set out to find Kermit.

They found Kermit in a fancy mansion.

He split his time between the house

and a nice lily pad at the local pond.

"Hi, ho!" Kermit greeted them.

Walter and Gary told him the problem.

"You have to save the theater!" Walter cried.

Kermit knew the only way to save the theater
was to do what the Muppets did best.
They had to put on a show!
He missed performing, anyway,
and he missed his friends.
"Come on," Kermit said.
"Let's get the Muppets together again!"

Kermit and his new friends hit the road
to find the other Muppets.
Most of them were happy to see Kermit.

But when they found Miss Piggy,

she was still upset with Kermit.

"Piggy, we need your help," Kermit told her.

"This is about the whole gang!" he said.

She shook her head.

"No, Kermie," she said.

"This is about just me and you."

She said good-bye to him again.

The gang went back to Hollywood
without Piggy.
Still, the show must go on.
Kermit put aside his sadness
and told the Muppets to practice.
They even hired someone
named Miss Poogy to replace Miss Piggy.
But things just did not seem right
without the real Miss Piggy there.
"All right, is everyone here?"
Kermit asked.

Suddenly the door to the theater swung open.

"Hold it right there!" It was Miss Piggy!

"You came back!" cried Kermit.

"There is only one Piggy, and she is *moi*!"

Miss Piggy said.

She shooed Miss Poogy away.

The night of the big show,

Kermit went to talk to Piggy.

"Piggy, I missed you and I need you,"

he told her. It was hard for him to say.

"Oh, Kermie," said Piggy with a happy sigh.

"It is time for our song!" said Kermit.

Kermit went onstage first.

He strummed his banjo and sang his song.

Miss Piggy walked out and sang along.

Performing side by side,

they knew they were meant to be together.

Everyone was smiling.

The Muppets were together again—all of them.

Even Walter got to be in the show.

After their big finish,

the gang burst out of the theater doors.

They were shocked to find
thousands of people cheering them on!
All their fans had seen the big show on TV.
The Muppets were thrilled that their show
had made all these other people happy, too.

TICKETS

It did not matter anymore
if the Muppets saved the theater.
As long as they performed together,
sharing their music and jokes,
Kermit and his friends were happy.
"You are my family," Kermit told them.
Then he turned to the crowd.
"And that's our show!" he cried. "Yaaaaay!!!"